P9-BZK-130

A House for Mouse

by Babs Shook
illustrated by Kathy Couri

All-Star Readers®

Reader's Digest Children's Books™
Pleasantville, New York • Montréal, Québec

A Note to Parents

Read to your child...

★ Reading aloud is one of the best ways to develop your child's love of reading. Read together at least 20 minutes each day.

★ Laughter is contagious! Read with feeling. Show your child that reading is fun.

★ Take time to answer questions your child may have about the story. Linger over pages that interest your child.

...and your child will read to you.

★ Follow cues from your child to know when he wants to join in the reading.

★ Support your young reader. Give him a word whenever he asks for it.

★ Praise your child as he progresses. Your encouraging words will build his confidence.

You can help your Level 1 reader.

★ Reading begins with knowing how a book works. Show your child the title and where the story begins.

★ Ask your child to find picture clues on each page. Talk about what is happening in the story.

★ Point to the words as you read so your child can make the connection between the print and the story.

★ Ask your child to point to words she knows.

★ Let your child supply the rhyming words.

Most of all, enjoy your reading time together!

—Bernice Cullinan, Ph.D.,
Professor of Reading, New York University

Published by Reader's Digest Children's Books
Reader's Digest Road, Pleasantville, NY U.S.A. 10570-7000 and
Reader's Digest Children's Publishing Limited,
The Ice House, 124-126 Walcot Street, Bath UK BA1 5BG
Copyright © 2000 Reader's Digest Children's Publishing, Inc.
All rights reserved. Reader's Digest Children's Books is a trademark and
Reader's Digest and All-Star Readers are registered trademarks of
The Reader's Digest Association, Inc. Fisher-Price trademarks are used
under license from Fisher-Price, Inc., a subsidiary of
Mattel, Inc., East Aurora, NY 14052 U.S.A.
©2000 Mattel, Inc. All Rights Reserved.
Printed in Hong Kong.
10 9

Shook, Babs.
A house for mouse / by Babs Shook ; illustrated by Kathy Couri.
p. cm. — (All-star readers. Level 1)
Summary: Several animals offer to let a little mouse live with
them, but he keeps searching until he finds just the right home.
ISBN 1-57584-383-8 (alk. paper)
[1. Mice Fiction. 2. Animals—Habitations Fiction. 3. Stories in rhyme.]
I. Couri, Kathryn A., ill. II. Title. III. Series.
PZ8.3.S55915Ho 2000 [E] — dc21 99-34957

I am a mouse,
a little mouse.

I need a house,
a little house.

I need a house,
a place to be.

I need a friend
to be with me.

A fish says, "Come.
Come live with me.

Come share my house.
It's in the sea."

I shake my head.

I say to him,
"I cannot come.
I cannot swim."

A bird says, "Come.
Come live with me.

Come share my house.
It's in a tree."

"Oh, dear!" I say,
"I cannot fly.
Your house is nice,
but it's too high."

And then I see
a little house.

It looks just right
for a little mouse.

And then I hear
somebody shout,
"Can you please come
and help me out?"

I go inside.
What do I see?

A little mouse—
a mouse like me.

He says, "I need
to paint my house.

But it's too hard
for just one mouse!"

"It's not too hard
for two," I say.

"I like to paint.
May I please stay?"

Today I am
a happy mouse.

I have a nice
new friend and house.

Color in the star next to each word you can read.

☆ a	☆ have	☆ may	☆ see
☆ am	☆ he	☆ me	☆ shake
☆ and	☆ head	☆ mouse	☆ share
☆ be	☆ hear	☆ my	☆ shout
☆ bird	☆ help	☆ need	☆ somebody
☆ but	☆ high	☆ new	☆ stay
☆ can	☆ him	☆ nice	☆ swim
☆ cannot	☆ house	☆ not	☆ the
☆ come	☆ I	☆ oh	☆ then
☆ dear	☆ in	☆ one	☆ to
☆ do	☆ inside	☆ out	☆ today
☆ fish	☆ is	☆ paint	☆ too
☆ fly	☆ it	☆ place	☆ tree
☆ for	☆ just	☆ please	☆ two
☆ friend	☆ like	☆ right	☆ what
☆ go	☆ little	☆ say	☆ with
☆ happy	☆ live	☆ says	☆ you
☆ hard	☆ looks	☆ sea	☆ your